The Balloon, Mount Tambura and the Flying Carpet

A wonderful adventure on the Apuan Alps.

By **Fernanda Raineri**

To those who have a dream.

PREFACE

The Versilia and the Apuan Alps are the main characters in this story, between reality and fantasy.

The four young protagonists find themselves in an enchanted forest on Mount Tambura, where mystery and adventure take control. It is a place where a priceless treasure is hidden. The characters will fly on the wings of imagination on the legendary "flying carpet".

Imagination is the primary source of human happiness.

Giacomo Leopardi

Imagination is more important than knowledge.

Albert Einstein

In San Carlo, a little town and spa resort, a few miles away from the Versilia Coast and the Apuan Alps, on the 1st of August, was really hot: 39 degrees in the shade and the humidity was 80%.

Stella hated the summer, because the hot weather made her weak and prevented her from moving freely – besides the fact that she had to work all day long, of course. She was locked up in that supermarket – smiling at the customers and at her boss even when she didn't feel like it – and at the end of the month she got rewarded with a meagre salary of 800 Euros, barely enough to keep her in her studies and help her parents, the Ravellis, and her younger sister, Glenda.

Her father, Sempronio, a huge man who weighted 95 kg, was a factory worker on the dole who sought to supplement his meagre wages getting up very early in the morning to unload crates of fruit for the local markets. Her mother, Perla, a slender, sickly woman, was a housewife. Her little sister, Glenda, a mass of black hair and eyes, five feet of wisdom beyond her age, had just left middle school.

They couldn't even afford a vacation, not even in the nearby Versilia.

Stella was so tired, and felt such an uncontrollable desire of freedom, to leave everything and everyone, just like that, out of the blue: parents, sister and her few friends; but that wish left her every night, as she wouldn't even dream to leave school. She wanted to get her high school degree, and then go to university. Her dream was to become a journalist or a writer: someday, she was sure, she'd reach her goal.

"Stella!" She had just arrived home, and her mom was already calling her. "Get the laundry and close the windows".

Of course, she always has something for me to do, the girl thought with a sigh. She'd have liked to check her emails first. She was waiting for her friends Rebecca and Frank, who lived in Boston, to get in touch; they were supposed to confirm their arrival in Italy and, especially, the balloon trip that they had planned the last time they had seen each other, around Easter.

Stella had not told her parents about it yet, because she already knew what they'd have said: that she was crazy, that only she'd get such ideas, that it was dangerous, all that stuff. Glenda, however, thought that that idea was just great.

The trip would only last two days, with a flight for each day. Stella had already applied for her holidays to her boss, and he had granted them, albeit reluctantly. It was going to be an exciting, wonderful experience. Balloons had always fascinated her, ever since she had read *Around the World in 80 Days* by Jules Verne for the first time.

"You know, mom? Stella will fly on a balloon?" said her sister at dinner, that night.

"On a balloon? What balloon? What do you mean, 'balloon'? " their father muttered, his mouth full of a delicious risotto.

"What?" her mother asked nervously.

"Yes, a balloon! You know, the hot air balloons that you sometimes see on the telly, when they have some international gathering? Didn't you read *Around the World in 80 Days*?" Stella said, trying to make it sound as normal as possible.

"What on Earth are you talking about? Are you kidding me?"

Their mother thought – and hoped – that it was one of the usual, weird ideas her daughter liked to share with them, one of the hundreds of things she said she'd do but never happened.

"No, I'm going, or at least I think I will: Rebecca and Frank haven't replied to my email yet. But if they are coming, we'll go".

"Oh well..." her father added, seeing that she seemed so sure about her decision. Stella was glad she had shown her determination. Usually, at home, she was just submissive. But not this time!

After dinner, she went finally managed to find the time to check her emails.

"Hooray!" Rebecca had confirmed it all in writing. Frank would take care of booking them all for the trip as soon as they arrived in Italy, on the 7th of August; she could even bring someone else, as there was room for one more person. The balloon would take flight from Bagni di Lucca, and the international gathering was to take place on the 15th and 16th. They would stay in Massa, at their aunt Mafalda's, for a few days, relaxing on the beach in Massa, before enjoying the balloon trip.

Frank and Rebecca's parents, the Giulianis, were Italian-American. Mr. Giuliani had moved to the USA after earning his degree in electrical engineering, and had found a job and a wife in Boston. Frank and Rebecca were born and raised in the U.S., but they often spent their holidays in Italy, at their aunt's. Mrs. Mafalda was an old friend of the Ravelli family. Before they got married, she and Glenda and Stella's mother had worked, at the spa in San Carlo; after quitting that job they had kept in touch.

So Frank and Rebecca had met the two sisters, and they had become friends.

Stella was over the moon: the trip would start not too far from home. At least this would have made her parents happy.

"Mom, it's organised! And we'll be leaving from a place nearby, are you happy?"

"No, I'm not, but if you are..." she replied with an unhappy tone. She wondered why Stella always asked for her parents' approval even when she knew they wouldn't give it.

"Glenda, listen: Frank told me there is room for another person on the balloon. Would you like to come with us? Otherwise I'll call Alfiero: Mrs. Biaggi's son; I know he flies gliders".

"What do gliders have to do with balloons?" her sister asked, amused.

"Well, they both fly without an engine, don't they?" Stella said.

"Mmh, right, forget it. Anyways, I can't answer now. You know I can't even get in an elevator, how do you think I'd be able to fly on a balloon?"

"Don't worry! Balloons are open, you can breathe the fresh air, it's not like being locked in an elevator!" said Stella, trying to tickle her sister's fancy for anything 'green'.

"Fine, fine, I'll think about it, I'll give you an answer tomorrow".

Glenda always needed to think about everything. Stella, instead, took her best decision on the spur of the moment.

The following day, her sister agreed to join them, and Stella immediately phoned Frank to confirm. It would be the four of them – five with the pilot. Fifteen days to go, and the girl just couldn't wait. Surprisingly, those days passed quickly. Finally, the time came.

"So, do we have everything?" Stella asked Glenda. "I have a yellow hat that matches my hair, sunglasses, my bag, my mobile of course, a windproof jacket and a survival kit I got as a gift, mostly because it contains binoculars so I can enjoy the view."

Her clothes were light: t-shirt and linen pants with big pockets, sneakers and socks. Glenda, was carrying and wearing more or less the same stuff. However, instead of a survival kit, she had taken some pills against air-sickness and, of course, her camera.

"We're going now, bye mom and dad, we'll call you from the sky".

Glenda reproached her sister. "Don't talk like that, Stella!"

"Why? What did I say?" she replied.

"I don't like how you've said it, it sounded… bad!" Glenda replied.

"Right then, bye mom, bye dad, we'll call you as soon as we hit the ground!"

They jumped on their scooters. Their parents waved at them with an expression that seemed to be suggesting that they were thinking *Where the Hell are you going? You really need to do this?*

Rebecca and Frank were waiting for them next to their motorbike. They were perfectly on time.

As soon as she saw them coming, the girl started waving her arms and jumping all over.

She looks like a cheerleader, Glenda thought.

Frank didn't move, but smiled. The sunlight was reflected by the retainer on his teeth; his eyes seemed to shine, too. It always happened, every time he saw Stella. His jokes, his cocky walk couldn't hide the fact that he had always been attracted by her.

"What do you have in that bag, a parachute?" said Frank.

"No, an airbag, just in case we crash", replied Glenda.

"What about you, Rebecca?" Stella wanted to know if bringing a windproof jacket had been overkill.

"I brought a cotton sweater and Frank… you know... one of those jackets with lots of pockets, for your mobile, your specs, your lighter..."

"Pretty much like wearing a bag then!" said the girl.

"What do you think, shall we go?" asked Frank. His gaze met Stella's. He hoped that his feelings would reach her without any need for words: talking about them would have been embarrassing. He hated himself for not being able to come forward, but he was too afraid to spoil what they already had.

Stella held his gaze, then looked at the sky saying: "Let's go, I don't want to be late".

Frank thought he had seen her blush just a little. He hoped it was true. "You're right, let's go".

His tone sounded stronger than ever. Maybe it was the emotion of the moment he had just shared with Stella.

What a traffic jam! Is everyone on holidays in the Versilia? Stella thought. She couldn't wait to get where they were going.

Finally they reached the gathering place.

"Wonderful! There must be at least fifty balloons!" said Glenda.

She immediately took a picture; it was a feast of colours in the middle of nature. They looked for their balloon which, since it could take five people, had to be one of the biggest. They had been told that the balloon was painted with red, green, yellow and white stripes on it. On the side, they'd immediately notice its name: *Nautilus*.

"Weird", Rebecca said. "That name would be more appropriate for a submarine, don't you think?"

"Oh shut up!" Stella replied. "Nautilus is also a shell".

"I didn't know. This explains everything then", said Glenda.

"Found it! Man, it's awesome!"

Stella was delighted. And the pilot was not bad looking either: young and handsome, he looked around twenty.

"Good morning everybody, ready to go?" the tall young man asked, in the local accent.

"Of course!" replied Stella with a smile that showed her big teeth. Rebecca and Glenda began to whisper to each other, exchanging opinions about the guy's tan – too perfect –and his age. They thought that someone so young couldn't have the experience needed to fly a balloon.

"Come on girls, if he's here he must be good, whatever his age", said Stella, trying to reassure her friends.

Frank seemed to agree: "What matters is that they have a lot of flying hours and experience: age doesn't matter."

"Right, my name is Alfredo, call me Alfred", the pilot said. They shook his hand, finding it slightly sweaty.

"Now, get in the basket one at a time, I'll help from the ground. You didn't bring any heavy luggage, right?"

"Of course not!" they all replied.

"Right. Get in, quick".

Alfred helped them all in. The friends looked at each other, smiling and a little excited. Frank cleared his throat and asked when they were going to take of.

"At 9 sharp, like the other balloons. We'll raise silently in this wonderful blue sky", answered Alfred. They checked their watches, without realising that there was one hanging from one of the ropes of the balloon. It was 8:55.

"Feel how fast my heart is beating", said Stella said, showing her wrist to Glenda and her friend.

"It's fear!" commented Frank with a smile.

"Hell no! I'm not afraid. I'm just very excited".

"Yeah, right, excited", said Rebecca.

The time came. One staff member cut the rope of the balloon. Alfred pulled a handle that made the blue flame more powerful. The four friends were clenching the ropes.

And then… up, straight, fast, light as feathers.

The feeling was impossible to describe. Seeing all those balloon raising silently from the ground, at the same time, and then move in different directions. As if they had escaped from the hand of a child.

"Very well guys, now we'll reach a height of 1,500 meters and, helped by the wind, we'll head to our destination, where someone will be waiting for us. We'll spend a couple of hours in the air before descending softly. In the meantime, enjoy the wonderful view of the Apuan Alps and our beautiful coast. Isn't it amazing?"

Alfred seemed extremely confident and trustworthy.

The friends started feeling more relaxed. Glenda started taking pictures of them, of Alfred, of the balloon and of the landscape. They continued to fly towards the mountains, moving with the coast behind them.

"Hey, guys! Why don't we call home and tell them that we're flying right above their heads? Look over there! That's the church, and there's our house!" Stella, who was watching in that direction with her binoculars, was euphoric.

"Let's", agreed Frank, and immediately took his mobile from his pocket.

Glenda was faster. "Hey, there's no signal!" she said. "Are yours working?"

Unfortunately, everyone noticed the same. Frank, annoyed, turned to Alfred and asked if it was normal.

"Well, that depends. Sometimes it's indeed impossible to get a signal up here. It depends on wind and on the magnetic waves. Anyway, don't worry: we are in contact with the event staff through this radio", he reassured them pointing at a receiver hanging on one of the ropes. "We use a specific VHF frequency".

The four friends didn't understand a word of what Alfred said, but he sounded so professional that they didn't ask any more questions and continued to enjoy the view. The landscape was wonderful. No noise except for the fire that kept the balloon flying and the flapping of the wings of some birds.

They were all silent, staring dreamily at the mountains and the sea. Stella thought that she'd have liked to go around the world on a balloon, but not in 80 days like in the book: she'd take her time.

"We're getting close to the Apuan Alps, specifically Mount Tambura", said Alfred. "See, Tambura is that ridge there, in the middle. It is 1,889 meters high, one of the highest peaks of the Apuans. We'll soon be able to see the vegetation covering the valleys."

Stella, in the meantime, was enjoying the view with her binoculars, that she then passed around.

"Stella, don't you think the wind has gotten stronger? We are moving faster, and my hair wasn't fluttering like this earlier", Glenda said while trying to keep her dark hair in place.

"Well, I don't think so, what about you guys?" said the elder sister, turning to Frank and Rebecca. Both shook their heads looking at Alfred, waiting for a confirmation.

"Damn it, the wind is indeed increasing", he said. "It's weird: the forecast only mentioned a light breeze". He grabbed the radio.

"Hello, Nautilus here, can you hear me?"

A few minutes passed in silence, waiting for an answer. Stella, Glenda, Rebecca and Frank were staring at the pilot without saying a single word.

"Yes, Nautilus, we can hear you."

Finally, a voice through the radio. The guys relaxed a bit.

"The wind has suddenly increased, I don't know if I'll be able to land in the agreed spot. Please give me directions for somewhere else to land".

That didn't feel right.

"Don't worry, we're following your progress from down here; we'll give you all the instructions you need".

These were the last words that the radio transmitted. The wind increased even more. It was like it wanted to push them away, against the Tambura; Alfred, silently, placed himself in front of the burner and grabbed the handle, trying to decrease the pressure thus slowing the balloon down. With the wind increasing, the balloon was taken by an air vortex and started to turn on itself.

"Hang on to the ropes!" Stella yelled. They were being tossed around like eggs in a basket, afraid to be scrambled.

The pilot realised that the burner had gone off and, shouting "Every man for himself!" clung to one of the steel cables – the same one Stella was holding. He tried to grab the radio again but, as soon as he managed to unhook it, it slipped from his hand and fell.

We'll end up the same, Stella thought. The balloon continued to twist and turn. And fall. None of them had the strength to scream. Stella felt her heart beating hard, and thought she was about to pee herself. The basket bounced on the top of a tree, then another. They all fell out.

When Stella woke up, she didn't know how much time had passed. Her face was on the ground, she could smell it, even taste it; she raised her head to spit some blades of grass. Strangely, she did not feel any pain: she was only a little sore and really shaken. She struggled to get up on her feet; her head was spinning.

"Glenda! Frank! Rebecca!"

She shouted the names of her friends, but nobody answered. No voices, no moans. Yet, they had been thrown out of the balloon at the same time, so they must be around somewhere. She continued calling their names, and Alfred's too.

"Where are you guys? Are you all alive?"

With all these trees and grass, they must have fallen on soft ground, she thought, trying to remain positive.

"Stella! We're here!"

Finally. She looked around, but she only could see green, deep and thick, made brilliant by the sunlight filtering through the trees.

"Hey! Shout louder, so I can find you!"

"Here!" they all yelled together.

Maybe she had understood where the voices were coming from: straight in front of her. She started walking in that direction, as fast as she could, while asking her friends to keep making noise so she could make sure she was on the right track.

"Hey! Here!" they continued.

Finally she saw them. They were all fine. She noticed that their clothes were dirty but, besides some scratches, nobody had been hurt.

Alfred was missing, though, and nobody seemed to have seen him.

"Guys, thanks God we're all safe! Now we need to look for Alfred", Rebecca said.

They decided to walk for about 50 meters, at a certain distance apart but still making sure they wouldn't lose eye contact, heading towards the spot where Stella had fallen; they would then explore the area where Glenda, Rebecca and Frank had fallen. They shouted Alfred's name a few times, but didn't get any answer. The pilot seemed to have disappeared.

Frank thought that probably Alfred was already walking on the Vandelli path out of the woods and maybe he had already reached the town. He'd be back soon with some help.

"Do you still have your mobiles? I can't find mine, it must have fallen somewhere", said Frank, touching his pocket.

They realised that only Stella still had hers, as Glenda had lost her whole bag. But it wasn't working, as there seemed to be no signal.

"What now? We've lost our mobiles, Alfred, the balloon and the radio. Who's going to find us?" complained Rebecca.

"Calm down girls", said Frank. "We can still walk, right? So, let's walk! It's 10:30 in the morning and we have plenty of time to find the right path to follow, the Vandelli maybe, or any other really: the Tambura is full of them".

"How can you be so sure we fell on the Tambura?" Glenda always seemed to be challenging Frank's confidence.

"I'm not 100%, but 80%".

"Admittedly, it's not as if we had anything else to rely on", admitted the girl.

They needed to find a way out before nightfall. First of all, though, they had to get out of the woods. It'd have been a good start. But how could they know what direction to take?

Stella suddenly remembered the small survival kit she was carrying in her bag; in it, she found a compass.

"That's it! This should be good for something", she said proudly.

"You're great, Stella!" said Frank taking the compass. "So, it shows that North is right in front of us, on the left we have the West, where the sun sets. The coast is there: the sun sets into the sea here, right? I'd suggest to go that way, then: so we'll begin to go down and there'll be more chances to find a path."

Stella, Glenda and Rebecca, however, didn't agree: they insisted that they should go East and climb; they thought that only by going up they'd get out of the woods.

But Frank was older – and bigger – than any of them, so they ended up following his suggestion. The boy became their leader.

They walked for about an hour and a half. It was noon, and they still weren't out of the woods. It could have been a fairy-tale forest, populated by fairies and gnomes: such was the atmosphere there, with the sunlight making its way through the majestic beech and chestnut trees, colouring the undergrowth and making the grass look golden.

Multicoloured butterflies fluttered in all directions, while beautiful birds, including green and red woodpeckers, rested on the branches. Occasionally, squirrels sneaked through the trees holding a nut in their small mouths. A doe trotted by without any fear, looking at them.

"Guys, let's take a break. I'm hungry and tired... actually, we're all tired and hungry", said Glenda, interrupting the magic. She sat on the grass, leaning against the trunk of a tree.

"Yes, you're right, let's rest for an hour", agreed Frank.

Stella, meanwhile, checked her mobile. Still no signal, and the battery was nearly flat.

"Our parents must be awfully worried! I'm sure, though, that they've been contacted and are already looking for us", she said.

"Everything will be fine, they'll find us soon", said Rebecca trying to reassure everybody.

Stella sat down on the grass and, looking around, saw some beautiful red fruits; they looked like small strawberries.

"Look what I found!"

"What?" Rebecca turned around.

"Here, look! Strawberries! And they are good!" she said, eating one.

They all began searching for more. Stella took off her hat and filled it completely with strawberries. They ate until they had enough.

"I hope we won't get a sore stomach", said Frank putting in his mouth the last, delicious strawberry.

Soon after, happy and refreshed, they restarted walking. Frank picked up a branch that he had found. It was strong and straight: he removed its leaves and made a stick.

"We can use it in case we see a snake – I know that around here you can find vipers. I'll hit the ground with every step I take, so I'll scare them off".

"Then we should all get one, don't you think?"

They started looking for some branches.

They walked in a line, making such a racket with their sticks to frighten any snake in the whole forest. With all the holes they had made by hitting the ground, they had unwittingly left tracks.

Suddenly, Frank stopped and pointed to the right, with his stick. Amazed, they saw, about 30 meters away, the basket of the balloon hanging from a tree. They got closer. They also saw the balloon itself, deflated, between the tree and the ground.

"How did it get here? We were thrown out about two hours' walk away from here!"

"Probably, after we fell, it continued to fly above the trees until the balloon got completely deflated and stopped there", Stella guessed; the others agreed..

Luck was on their side. Near the balloon, they found Glenda's purse with all its contents, including a box of cookies and a bottle of water that she had brought with her.

Frank got the idea to pull down the Nautilus: it would be useful as a shelter.

"Maybe it'd be better if we stop here, if the ground crew has followed our flight they definitely know where the Nautilus has fallen, so this is where they will start looking. I suggest we use the basket as a shelter, just in case they don't find us before nightfall".

Stella, however, had another idea: "Why don't we use the basket to light a fire, so they can see the smoke? Like this, they'll see us immediately".

Her sister agreed, but Rebecca didn't: "Sure, let's burn the wood down, so they'll find us chargrilled!"

Frank thought it dangerous too: "I'd rather not play with fire, not in the woods".

They decided against the fire, and tried to understand how to bring the balloon down. They soon realized that was impossible: its four ropes were trapped in the branches of a big chestnut tree, and the basket was hanging about two metres off the ground.

They agreed that Frank, who was pretty tall – 1.80, despite being only fifteen – would stand under the basket, and one of the girls would climb on his shoulders trying to check if it was firmly attached to the tree and able to hold their weight. It seemed solid, but it's better to be safe than sorry.

Stella climbed on the boy's shoulders, who staggered a little under her weight. Glenda and Rebecca stood either side of Frank to support him, in case he lost his balance.

"Right, a little further... I might be able to grab the edge of the basket… there!"

Frank pushed her up to help her in.

"It seems very solid. And there's a rope here, it may be useful", said Stella, throwing it to her friends.

"We could use it to make a ladder, so we wouldn't need to climb on Frank's shoulders", said Glenda.

"Good idea! We need some pieces of wood to make pegs", added Rebecca.

Frank put himself to the task. With the help of the utility knife that Stella carried in her survival kit, he broke the sticks the girls had found into four parts. Using those as pegs, he created a small ladder. They only needed to attach it securely to the basket. Frank tossed it to Stella, who secured it to a big hook.

"Who's going up first?" asked the girl. Her sister immediately volunteered and, struggling a little, managed to get up, followed by the others.

The Nautilus had gotten stuck on a huge chestnut tree that seemed ancient, and didn't appear to have any issues supporting their weight. The friends were elated for what they had managed to do – and for having found their hot air balloon.

In the meantime, rescuers had already been looking for them for several hours. Their parents, frightened, waited for news. The next day the story would surely be all over the news.

Meanwhile, the sun began to disappear. The four friends were beginning to lose hope of being found before the end of the day.

Slowly, the light that embroidered the thick foliage of the trees died down. Everything seemed different then: the enchanted woods became dark, hostile, and the shapes of the trees seemed threatening. The friends heard strange noises and animal voices – probably owls – which made the darkness seem even more sinister.

It was getting cold, too. The friends were huddled in the basket, keeping each other warm.

Rebecca jumped. "Oh my God! The…there's a lot of yellow eyes out there! They're watching us!"

"Just some nocturnal animals looking for food", Frank whispered.

"You know, I read some legends about Mount Tambura: witches, demons and ghosts", said the girl.

"Are you trying to frighten us?" said Stella.

"…just legends", intervened Glenda.

"Definitely!" Frank said. "Although, I read in the paper about a UFO sighting. Two witnesses reported red lights in the sky, moving from the mountains towards the coast. There are witnesses, so it must be true", he said with a mysterious look on his face.

A branch broke nearby. The noise of something moving through the leaves.

"Did you hear that?" said Rebecca.

"Must have been one of those… animals, just walking around", said Glenda.

"Bu… but… but… it's ge… getting nearer!"

"Reb, please… calm down", said Frank.

"Le… le… le… leave m… me alone!"

Stella tried to defuse the situation. "Rebecca, calm down, everything's fine. Frank, you aren't helping".

The boy turned the other way: being scolded by Stella was hard for him. He immediately started thinking of how to get back on her good side.

"Ste… Stella?" said Rebecca

"I'm here".

Rebecca took her hand. "I'm.. f… f… f… frightened…"

"It's normal, don't worry, everything will be fine".

"I c… c… can't… b… buh… breathe…"

"Listen to me: nothing and nobody can harm us".

"Buh… but I…"

"Stella, please, do something". Glenda's voice was breaking, too. Stella knew that fear is contagious and, if her friends had panicked, the situation would degenerate fast.

She searched in her bag, as capacious as Mary Poppins's, and found a tiny flashlight, similar to those doctors use to examine their patients' throats. She switched it on, and that tiny ray of light seemed to change the whole situation. It was as if whatever weighted down on them had disappeared. Rebecca started breathing normally.

And then, Frank had the idea he had been looking for.

"Stella, can you make the beam wider?"

"Sure, why?"

"Please do it".

Stella did what Frank had asked her.

"Now, could you please stand up and point the torch down?"

"Yes, but… why?"

"Trust me".

Their eyes met for an instant: enough for Stella to notice some satisfaction in Frank's face.

The beam covered the whole floor of the basket.

Frank's hands started moving in the light. Those long fingers, so used to score on the basketball court, gave life to wonderful animal shapes. First it was an eagle, then a dinosaur, finally an elephant, trunk and all.

Rebecca smiled.

Stella, instinctively, said "You're great!"

Glenda shared some of her cookies; they ate them together, enjoying that magical show.

In town, meanwhile, everybody was talking about Frank, Glenda, Stella and Rebecca; nobody knew if they were still alive, as there had been no radio contact since the balloon had fallen. Everybody knew that a rescue operation would have been extremely challenging in those areas: several hikers had been lost there in the past.

The people were all gathered around the families, helping and supporting as much as they could, telling them that the four friends would surely be found, perfectly fine, very soon.

At dawn, Stella was awakened by a ray of sunlight that, through the woven basket, seemed to kiss her eyelashes. She felt its warmth. So she woke the others who, complaining about the position in which they had been forced to sleep, seemed to struggle to open their eyes, as if they been sealed.

Once they were all awake they finished Glenda's cookies. Then they decided to leave the basket and move eastwards, using the compass. They picked up their few belongings, the two sticks that hadn't been used for the ladder and started walking.

While they were walking, Frank told Stella that, during the night, he had been awakened by the sound of footsteps in the grass: steps that had stopped just below them and then had moved away quickly. He couldn't tell if it had been a person or an animal, but one thing was certain: if that was an animal, it must have been a big one.

"It could have been a wild boar, or the deer we had met earlier", she suggested.

They decided to keep that a secret, to make sure their younger sisters didn't get frightened and what had happened the previous night didn't happen again.

At a certain point, Rebecca told them that she had the feeling that someone was following them: "I heard something moving behind us, close by those ferns, and it was definitely not the wind. I felt watched".

"I'm sure it was some man-eating beast. It saw you, it's keeping an eye on you, and at the right time... you'll be its dinner!" Frank teased her.

"Come on, Rebecca! Don't be silly. Who do you think it can be? It's only us, the trees and some small animals. Look, isn't it beautiful?" said Stella, firmly.

"Hey, look over there, can you see it? There's a hillock, maybe it means that we are out of the woods!" said Frank.

Stella took a closer look with her binoculars. It was true.

They got out of the wood to find themselves in a green valley covered with bushes and grass. Further on, a waterfall formed a small stream, that ran through the valley.

They were all elated.

Fresh water, finally! They drank, washed their face and hands and played with the water. Then they ate the fruits that Glenda and Stella had gathered in the woods.

They sat down, at the feet of the hillock they had noticed earlier, sure they were near to a beaten path. After a few minutes, they heard a hum. They realized that it was the sound of a helicopter. Finally, someone had found them!

They all stood up, eyes turned to scan the clear sky. They continued to hear the noise, but there was no trace of the helicopter. They kept staring until they heard it leave.

"What the... Why didn't they come this way?" said Frank.

"They must have seen the balloon, and now they'll be heading there", said Rebecca, annoyed.

"Sure, and the rescue team will be heading there, too", added Glenda.

Stella added her opinion: "At this point it's better to wait here. If we go back, we may get lost: those woods are like a labyrinth. Let the rescue team come to find us: they know these mountains inside out, they'll find us".

She had hardly finished speaking when suddenly, from the top of the hillock, two large boulders came rolling down.

"Watch out!" Stella yelled.

The friends jumped away, frightened, and the boulders fell right where they had been seating.

"How did they come off?" said Frank, visibly upset. "They almost fell on our heads!"

To make sure they didn't run any further risk, they decided to go sit somewhere else. Frank, however, wanted to check the hillock first, and asked Stella if she wanted to go with him. Glenda and Rebecca told him that they refused to be left alone, and followed them.

The hillock was about 500 meters wide and 20 metres high: it wouldn't take them a long time to walk all around it.

While walking, they kept watching the top, to avoid unpleasant surprises. After about 200 meters, a fox darted between their legs, scaring them once again. Rebecca almost fell on the ground.

The small animal slipped into a slot just above them and disappeared.

Frank, curious, wanted to check where the fox had hidden. The girls followed him, although with some hesitation. They climbed a little, close to the mound and arrived at the point where the fox had disappeared. They found the hole: it was tiny, barely big enough for a fox. They peered inside, but it was dark and they couldn't see anything; Stella then remembered about her little flashlight.

Still they couldn't see much. Anyway, there was no trace of the fox. That meant that the hole didn't end there. They looked for another entrance.

Tracing the outside of the hole with her hand, Stella notices that what she was touching wasn't part of the hill: it was a large stone, that seemed to be a door to something. No one would have been able to detect it without a careful examination of the surroundings.

"Hey, look at that!" said Stella, her eyes open wide like a cat's. "Someone must have put this stone here!"

It couldn't have been bigger than 1 metre and 80 centimetres. They probably could move it. They decided to try, two on one side and two on the other.

"I'll count to three, then we'll push it down that way. Agreed?" said Frank

The stone wasn't as heavy as they had thought, and they managed to roll it away.

They found themselves in front of the entrance of a tunnel. The sunlight didn't penetrate it in depth, leaving most of it in the shade. As soon as they stepped inside, going down something that seemed to be a step, the tunnel widened: it was about 1 meter wide and 2 high. They looked at each other in wonder.

"I'm n… not going in th… there", said Rebecca.

"Yes, I agree", added Glenda, nearly apologetic.

"Come on girls, what do you want to do, go back? Back, where?"

"Frank, don't give them all the burden of a fear we all share… don't tell me you are not afraid at all".

How could Stella always be right about him? And how was she able to tell him off so nicely?

When someone, anyone told him he was wrong, normally he got mad. But she was different.

Maybe it was one of the secrets hidden in that small word that had been flying around in their heads for quite some time. A mystery people called love.

"True, I'm not fully confident, but… we should stick together, right?"

"On this he's right, girls…"

Encouraged by Stella's support, Frank carried on. "Think about it: if the two of you remained here alone, wouldn't it be even more dangerous?"

"Well… true…", Glenda said. "What do you think, Reb?"

"I… I… I th… th… th… think… it s… s… seems easy now…"

Glenda touched her shoulder and spoke in the softest tone she could muster. "Nothing can happen to us if we stick together. We need to find a way to get out of here".

Rebecca nodded. "L… let's go. I… hate you". Despite her words, her face opened in a smile.

They started walk in the cave.

"We… we're g… going down", said Rebecca.

"True. Don't you think we should stop?" suggested Glenda.

Frank stopped any discussion. "We have no other choice".

They all felt that was the truth, so they kept walking down.

The sunlight was not lighting their steps any longer. Thankfully, they still had the small flashlight, but didn't know how much longer it'd last.

They walked for about fifteen minutes along the passage that sloped gently down.

Suddenly, they found themselves in front of a spectacular view that left them all in awe: they were in a large cave, and in the middle of it there was a small lake fed by an underground river. Streams flowed into several tunnels of different sizes.

From a large slit at the top, the sunlight penetrated the interior of the cave. Huge limestone stalactites were coming down from the ceiling; some of them met the stalagmites below to form columns making the cavern look like a natural temple. The lake had green and blue shades. They didn't need the torch anymore.

"It is wonderful! I wonder why the entrance has been closed", said Stella.

"Yes, it's weird, such a place should become a tourist attraction; why are they keeping it hidden?" agreed Frank.

Meanwhile, Rebecca and Glenda were walking on the edge of the lake, admiring the reflections of the water on the walls of the cave. Frank joined them; Stella, however, had stopped to watch the crystal-clear pool, in which trout were swimming. Suddenly, she noticed something shining in the water. It was something small and round. She picked it up.

"Guys, look what I found!"

It was a coin in perfect conditions. On it, there was an engraving of a man's face surrounded by the name *Alberico I Cybo Malaspina*. They couldn't believe it! A sixteenth century golden coin!

They didn't know whether to be glad or worried about finding it, as it probably explained the reason why the entrance to the cave was blocked by that stone.

"Looks like nobody has been here for several centuries, otherwise this coin would be in someone's pocket. The stone was almost welded to the wall by a moss and grass, nobody has gone through that passage recently", said Frank.

"True!" Glenda agreed.

"I remember reading on a history book that, when the Cybo Malaspina family ruled the area, the mountains were full of highwaymen who robbed anyone who ventured on the road from the Grand Duchy of Massa to Modena, the Vandelli path: that's why it stopped being used. Probably this was one of their hideouts", said Stella.

"There might be more coins, let's check the lake," said Rebecca, curious.

They decided to look near the shore first.

They didn't find anything, so Frank volunteered to venture in the water: he was the tallest, he said.

"Man, it's freezing! But gold is worth a cold!"

He found out that the water was not more than a meter deep, so the girls decided to join him. The bottom was rocky and slippery – and Stella slipped.

"Stella, Stella!" her friends screamed. Before they could help her up, she saw a box closed by a rusty padlock.

As soon as her head emerged, she said: "I saw something, maybe a box... man, it's cold!"

Rebecca and Glenda tried to help her dry with a cotton sweater. Meanwhile Frank, checking the bottom of the small lake, found the box Stella was talking about and lifted it. It wasn't very big, but it was quite heavy, and he struggled to bring it out of the water. It was made of dark gray wood, almost completely rotten, and there was a faded inscription on it.

"It's German", Glenda said. "I don't know what that means, but it's definitely German".

They wanted to see what was inside. Frank kicked the lock, which broke. The chest opened.

It was full of ammunition, apparently dating back to World War II! What did 1940s ammo have to do with a sixteenth-century coin?

He felt he had to continue to check under the lake before the sun went down. They seemed to have forgotten all about being rescued, their parents or the hunger. For nearly two days they had only eaten strawberries and some cookies, but they were too busy in that "treasure hunt" and nothing could distract them.

They decided to keep searching under the lake. Two went right and two left; they would move from the shore, meeting in the centre.

"Here!" Frank and Rebecca yelled.

Stella and her sister, the water up to their waist, struggled towards them. Frank had found another case, bigger than the first. The writing and the colour were the same. They lifted it together and took it out of the water; it wasn't locked. They opened it, and were disappointed when they found it contained only weapons: machine guns, clearly dating from the same period of the ammo.

They explored the rest of the lake, but they couldn't find anything else.

"Let's go get dry under that", said Rebecca pointing at the slot the sunlight came through.

The sun was warm on their clothes.

"Listen, I was thinking… the fox we saw; where is it? If it isn't here, maybe it means that there's another way out, don't you think?" said Stella.

"Makes perfect sense", said Frank. "So, rather than focussing on our treasure hunt, now we'll go fox hunting!"

The sun was really warm, and their clothes were already nearly dry. They started looking for the animal. They went inside that forest of natural columns, looking for some kind of hole on the walls. A few meters from where the little river left the cave, they found a tunnel about 30 centimetres wide; maybe that was the fox's burrow.

"Probably it just hid there, waiting for us to leave", Frank said.

"I'd suggest to give up and go back where we came from, we found something anyway", Stella added, showing the coin.

They headed to the exit. Stella was looking around one last time when, just opposite to where they were, she saw a small, ginger animal running through the rocks and disappearing again.

"I saw it! It was there!" she yelled.

To get there, they went around the lake. They moved quickly, balancing on the rocky and slippery ground.

"Where did it go? It was here!" Stella continued.

Then, right behind a stone column, they found a hole. It was big enough for them to walk through. On the ground they saw was a sign, a vertical line.

"What do you think it means?" asked Rebecca.

"Maybe it's a signal to mark this passage", said Stella.

Frank agreed.

"Maybe it's a Roman numeral", said Glenda.

"Well, maybe if we go in we'll find out", concluded Frank.

The passage was darker than anything they had ever seen.

"Gle… Glenda?"

"What's it, Reb?"

"I… I love you".

"Hey, you're not on death row!"

"Ca… can't I te… te… tell you how I f… f… f… feel?"

"Reb, you're mental. But that's one of the reasons why I love you".

Frank intervened: "If the ladies are done with this episode of their soap opera, maybe we can go…"

"Frank!" Stella hit his arm with a friendly slap.

"Right, right, only joking. Come on, let's go face our final destiny".

"Idiot".

"Clown".

"Go first, then! Here's my flashlight", said Stella.

The passage was about ten meters long.

"I hope the b… b… battery doesn't go f… flat right now!" said Rebecca, shivering. They were all thinking about the same thing.

"I still have a lighter", Frank reassured them.

They got to the end of the passage that let into a smaller, dark cave. Frank pointed the flashlight to the right and saw more crates, very similar to those they had found in the water; on top of one of them, there were some lanterns.

"Look! Oil lamps!" said Frank.

He took out his lighter and lit three. He kept one for himself and gave the others to Stella and Rebecca.

They looked around, and all screamed at the same time. In front of them, they saw two human skeletons. One was seating on one of the cases; its back to the wall, it was wearing a

German uniform and had a gun in its right hand. In the frontal part of its cranium there was a hole, likely caused by a bullet.

A little further away in front of it, another skeleton was on the floor, and it was also holding a gun in its right hand. There was an officers' hat not far from its head.

The four friends clung to each other.

They stayed like that, like frozen, holding the lanterns, for quite some time.

Then they shook themselves and kept looking around. The cave was full of cases, some closed and others open, that didn't contained ammo or weapons, but rather all kinds of jewels: necklaces, bracelets, earrings, rings, and even a tiara encrusted with diamonds. There were several gold bars and cups set with precious stones. They looked ancient: perhaps they had been stolen from a museum or a church. One of the trunks contained some rolled up sheets of canvas. They unrolled one. It was a painting, dated July 15, 1550. It was signed, but they couldn't decipher the handwriting. It was clearly ancient, valuable.

Then, with Stella's knife, they opened one of the locked chests. It was full of golden coins with the effigy of King Victor Emmanuel III of Italy. They also found a thick wad of green 50 Lira notes dated 1943, accompanied by some 500 Lira notes printed in the same year.

The crates contained things that were not only valuable, but also historically relevant. There were even some oriental rugs including a huge one that, despite all those years in the cave, was in very good conditions. Rolled in it there was a parchment, that Stella opened, curious to see what was written in it. She opened it and realised that it was in a language she couldn't understand. She showed it to the others.

"It could be Arabic", Rebecca said. "Along with the carpet… those signs remind me of the writing inside Mosques".

"Too bad nobody here knows Arabic", said Stella putting the parchment back where it was.

While they were inspecting the cases they kept looking at the two skeletons, as if they were afraid that they could stand up at any moment.

"Looks like they killed each other, probably because of the treasure", said Glenda.

"And what do you think happened to the others? This stuff can't have been carried in here by two men only ".

"One day my grandfather, who lived in this area during the war, told me about the Gothic line that crossed this very mountains", said Stella. "It was the theatre of several battles between the Germans and the freedom fighters. When the Nazis left, they hid most of the things they had stolen in caves like this one, to ease their retreat. But they never came back. Actually, it's said that some of the soldiers got lost and never came out of the caves".

"Who knows, maybe the rest of their squad died in battle", said Frank.

Stella, in the meantime, had moved closer to the skeleton on the ground. "Hey, guys! It's holding something in its hand!"

Frank, Glenda and Rebecca left the crates and moved closer.

"I don't dare to touch it, it gives me the creeps", Stella said

Frank and Rebecca tried to turn the skeleton on its back. Its mouth was wide open and showed fake teeth, amongst which a big slug was crawling. By looking at its uniform they realised that the man had been shot to the heart.

Frank pulled up the skeleton's left arm and Rebecca, with some reluctance, tried to open its hand of the poor man, but it was clenched so tight that she ended up snapping two of its fingers.

"Sorry!" she said. "Look, another coin, just like the one we found in the water".

Hoping to find more, they opened all the crates, but couldn't see any.

"So, what do we do now?" said Glenda. "We found a treasure, two dead bodies and two golden coins. I suggest we keep the money and get out of here. Let's go back where we came from and wait for someone to come find us. By the way, I'm starving".

Frank agreed with her, and so did Stella and Rebecca. Before they left, though, Glenda remembered she had a camera with her, and took some pictures.

They brought the lanterns with them; maybe they'd come useful. While they were leaving the smaller cave, they heard a noise behind their backs. They turned suddenly, frightened: it was only the fox. Its burrow was in a corner of that cave. They went to check and found two cubs.

"Look!" said Rebecca.

"Don't get too close, you don't want their mother to get angry", said Stella.

A fish bone near the burrow reminded them about the trout in the small lake. They were so hungry they could eat them raw! They decided to go back there and try to catch some. Frank got in the water, then he stopped and waited for the right moment, holding his stick like a javelin – and he caught one!

"Here's dinner!" he said.

It was pretty big, and they couldn't wait to eat it. They grilled it on one of the lanterns

"Tastes awesome", muttered Frank.

"Never eaten anything so good!" agreed Glenda.

Hungry as they were, probably they'd have enjoyed even a roasted shoe.

Stella and Rebecca remained silent: they were too busy eating. At the end of the meal, they washed their hands in the lake.

Rebecca went to have a drink of water. As soon as she got to the small stream that came out of a wall of the cave, the others saw her turn abruptly towards the dark side of the cave and then run back towards them. They sprang to their feet, alarmed.

"What's wrong?" asked her brother, worried.

"The…there was someone there! I s… saw a shadow on the wall, on the left. It... yes, it l… looked like a man in uniform, I saw the hat, looked like the dead officer's, I swear I saw him!" said Rebecca.

After a moment of silence, all tried to reassure her and calm her by saying that they were alone, sharing the cave only with the two corpses and a fox. Probably the shadow of some stalagmite had played a joke on her nerves.

"Right, let's get out of here!" said Stella.

As soon as she finished speaking, a mysterious figure emerged from the shadows, right where Rebecca insisted she had seen a shape. It wore a German officer's uniform and was holding a gun; the friends couldn't see its face and hands. They were all frightened, began to scream and ran towards the passage leading to the exit.

They managed to run in the dark without a flashlight. When they finally got outside, they kept running as if someone was following them. They only stopped when they reached the creek. Half an hour passed before any of them could find the strength to say something.

"What was that? *Who* was that?" said Glenda, her voice breaking.

"I don't know, I don't believe in ghosts", answered Frank.

Stella couldn't speak yet, her heart was still beating fast and she felt as if someone was choking her.

Then, all of a sudden, she realized something: "Damn! The coins! I left them all in there… and my bag too!" Her voice was back, as if by magic. "We have to go back." She continued.

Glenda, Rebecca and Frank looked at each other, surprised; since they got so scared, they thought it'd be better for all of them not to go back inside. Stella tried to persuade them that it was the right thing to do: she wanted to recover what she had found and discover what kind of mystery was behind that vision.

"You and Frank can go", Rebecca said. "Glenda and I will wait for you here".

"Again?" said Frank.

"Hadn't we agreed to stick together?" Stella pointed out.

"T… true, but after wh… wh… what we saw, we'd rather s… s… s… stay here. We have n… no intention to go even close to the hillock", said her sister.

Glenda, practical as usual, concluded: "You are our older brother and sister: aren't you supposed to protect us?"

"What the…" commented Stella.

"Let's show them what us old guys can do, then", said Frank taking her by the arm.

Stella drew closer to him saying: "Good point. Let's go".

They marched, comically, back to the cave, their heads held high. Stella clung to Frank, clutching her stick with the other hand.

Their hips were touching. That gave both some marvellous feelings, the possibility of further contact… some ideas that Frank had been nurturing for some time invaded Stella's mind.

They looked around warily, trying to make as little noise as possible. They were both trembling with fear, but determined to press on.

There was only one lantern left. The others were gone, and the bag too.

"The ghost must have taken them", said Stella.

They also noticed a black ski mask and a pair of gloves of the same colour.

"What are these?" Frank said. They began to realize that what they had seen was very likely not a ghost. Probably someone had worn the German officer's uniform to scare them away!

They went back to Glenda and Rebecca to tell them what they had seen. They decided to join them in search of the "ghost".

"It's four of us, and he's just one: he can't scare us again!" Frank said, looking like a super hero.

Even the girls agreed. "Of course!" continued Stella. "I still remember some *aikido* moves I have learned a few months ago".

Rebecca and Glenda, hearing her words, immediately took some sticks to use as *bokken*.

They went back in the cave, approaching, cautiously and stealthily, what they had started to think of as the "vault".

As they approached its entrance, hearing some footsteps, they hid between the dark stalagmites.

The man who had frightened them appeared, still wearing the uniform. This time, however, he wasn't holding the gun, but a lantern. They couldn't see his face. Then they saw him disappear on the other side.

When they were sure enough that he had left, they came out of their hiding place and reached the treasure cave, where they found Stella's bag. In addition, the parchment which had been wrapped inside the oriental rug was now laying on one of the many boxes; on a piece of paper, someone had translated it into Italian. The mystery was thickening.

They took the bag, the translation and the carpet which, oddly enough, was as light as a feather despite its size. They left in a hurry.

They went back to the dark corner they had been hiding in and began to read at the light of the lantern. Unbelievable! The inscription talked about a "flying carpet", clearly the one they had brought with them. The carpet, it said, was magical and belonged to a sultan of Kuwait who had given one of his twelve sons, for his twelfth birthday. Sitta, that was his name, was a boy with a vivid imagination, who liked to write stories; one of them was about a magic carpet that flew with the power of the imagination of those who owned it.

With our imagination we create new worlds, it can even make you fly.

So fly, tell the carpet where to go.

No need to talk, just imagine.

If you use your imagination well, you can get wherever you want.

But remember: when the sun falls, the carpet will fade and go back where it belongs.

After reading the translation of the parchment, they looked at each other in amazement.

"What is it? A riddle?" said Rebecca.

"This is stupid", said Frank. "Since when flying carpets are real? They only exist in fairy tales".

"The carpet looks really very old, though, it's frayed and a little yellow, and the drawings suggest it's really oriental", Glenda said, excited.

While they were talking, in low voices, about the carpet, they heard footsteps again. Instantly they fell silent and turned off the lantern.

It was the man who had frightened them earlier. He was carrying two bags. This time they could see his face. Glenda recognized him and was about to yell his name, but Frank was fast enough to cover her mouth with his hand. Alfred! It was Alfred, their pilot. How was that possible? Where did he come from? When did he get to the cave? A thousand questions crowded their heads. They thought he had gone home!

They followed him from a distance while he was heading to the cave with the treasure. They wanted to see what he had in those two bags. He turned his back to the entrance. He was picking up coins from the bags and throwing them in the air, laughing and screaming some weird words in a strange language, probably Arabic. Sure he was the one who had translated the paper.

"I told you guys he looked too tanned!" Glenda whispered. "He definitely has Middle-Eastern origins".

Alfred kept throwing the coins in the air, jumping round and smiling: he seemed to have lost his mind. They left him alone and went in the opposite direction, where they had seen him coming from.

Behind another big calcareous column, another passage was hidden. On the ground, another sign was carved: two vertical bars, similar to the number 2 in Roman numerals.

"Look, this means that this one is the second cave, the one we were in earlier must be the first. I wonder if there are also a third and a fourth!" said Frank, intrigued.

"Guys, let's go, quick! I don't want to wait for Alfred to come back this way. When he'll realise that my bag and the carpet are gone he might get mad", said Stella.

"Yes, it's true, let's go, we need to hurry", Glenda agreed.

Silently, they entered the passage, which was more or less as long as the other, and reached the entrance of the second cave. There, they saw something glittering in the dark, but couldn't tell what it was.

Frank noticed two wooden torches to the sides of the entrance, and tried to light one of them. He saw that it still worked despite the long time it sure had been there, so they lighted the other one too.

"Oh gosh!" they all said.

The cave was full of bags and chests, full of gold and silver coins. The former were similar to those Stella had in her bag, while the silver ones showed on one side the head of Alberico I Cybo Malaspina, and on the other the image of three deer.

Other chests contained jewels, certainly ancient. Everybody felt the need to sink their hands in all those coins.

"Now I understand why those two Germans have been killed. Probably all this gold had the same effect it had on Alfred", said Frank.

"This is what I was talking about, the bandits!" added Glenda.

"Yes, And all this has been here for centuries until, during the Second World War, while they were retreating, the German troops found this cave, and probably decided to use it to hide what they had taken from the nearby cities, too. Sure they planned to come back, but most likely, the people who knew about this are all dead", Stella said, playing with some coins.

Glenda pulled out her digital camera and took some pictures.

They stayed for a while, discussing what to do next and contemplating that wonderful treasure, completely forgetting about Alfred. They couldn't decide whether to take a few bags or not: they seemed afraid to steal what had been stolen, and also had the feeling of desecrating something. But, suddenly, a roar startled them.

"What was that? Did the roof cave in?" Glenda shouted in panic.

"Calm down, let's go find out what happened", said Stella, pretending not to be frightened.

They cautiously went out of the cave. Everything seemed quiet, there was no trace of Alfred and there were no signs of any collapse. They noticed, however, some smoke, or maybe it was dust from the corridor that led outside. Stella had a bad feeling.

"Guys, it's better if we head towards the exit, even though I have the feeling that we'll find a nasty surprise there", she said.

And a nasty surprise was really waiting for them: part of the ceiling had caved in, and the passage that led outside was completely closed by a number of boulders. There was a strange smell in the air that reminded them of firecrackers, like those blown for New Year. It was definitely gunpowder.

"What do we do now? How will we get out of here?" said Frank.

"We'll be stuck in here forever! Alfred has taken off with some of the treasure, trapping us in here!" said Rebecca.

"We need to find the explosives he used. They must be where the ammo are", said Stella, proactively.

They went back to the first cave, where another nasty surprise awaited them: everything was still there, even the two bags of golden coins that Alfred had taken there. So he hadn't left! But why would he trap himself in there? Perhaps, simply, there was another way out! While they wondered where Alfred could be, they got interrupted by a new explosion.

"What's happening now?" Glenda screamed. They ran back to the lake, through the dark passage. They saw black smoke coming from the second cave; when it faded away, they realized that the entrance was completely blocked by rocks: he had brought everything down!

In that moment, Alfred appeared right before their eyes. As soon as he saw them, he started to yell, holding a dynamite stick in one hand and a torch in the other. Around his neck, he carried a sack of gunpowder.

"Damn you all! If the treasure can't be mine, nobody will have it!"

He kept spouting gibberish interspersed by some Italian and, probably, some Arabic; at the same time, he lit the dynamite stick and threw it towards them.

Thankfully, the dynamite stick fell short and exploded in the pond, raising a lot of water. They were terrified and didn't know what to do. Then they saw more explosives coming. Frank showed his baseball skills and hit the dynamite with his stick, sending it back to where it came from. Alfred, frightened, jumped in the water to avoid it.

The dynamite exploded before it reached the ground. Some stalactites snapped and fell in the lake. The four friends took advantage of the commotion to hide but, strangely, they didn'tt see Alfred resurface. They waited for several minutes.

"He's trying to trick us. I bet he's just waiting for us to move so he can attack us", whispered Glenda, staring at the water still shaken by the explosion. They waited a little longer, but it seemed that Alfred had disappeared again.

"It's impossible that he can hold his breath for so long! Maybe he's passed out, or even died", said Frank. After a few seconds, he stood up. He walked to the shore and watched the lake; he realised that nobody was there. So he gestured his friends to come closer.

"Maybe we should get inside to take a look", Stella said, turning to Frank. "If he's dead, he probably is at the bottom of the lake". She didn't take her eyes off the boy, who had already understood that she was expecting him to volunteer for the task.

"Sure, but we have to do it the same way we did with the golden coins: all together!"

Stella, Glenda and Rebecca nodded reluctantly and, with a little bit of concern, they got into the cold water with Frank. They advanced slowly towards the point where they had seen Alfred diving and from there they started walking slowly, not to make any noise, looking everywhere.

They found no trace of Alfred's body nor of the bag of dynamite.

"He can't have just disappeared", said Stella.

"…and the fish can't have eaten him", added Glenda, pointing at a beautiful trout that swam before their eyes.

One more mystery, Stella thought to herself.

"He could be in one of those tunnels through which the water flows out of the lake, there's one big enough there", said Frank, trying to give a logical solution to the disappearance of Alfred's body.

"Yes, but it can't have been easy to end up there", replied Rebecca.

Frank noticed that his sister hadn't stuttered. He was proud of that, and tried to show it with a look: he sure couldn't start saying cheesy stuff in front of everyone.

"What? Is there something on my face?" said Rebecca wiping her cheeks.

"Eh? Oh, no… it's nothing".

Frank realised that his non-verbal communication was not exactly great, so he decided to focus on something he seemed to be better at: save his own life. Alfred couldn't have just disappeared like that, and definitely hadn't emerged from the lake: from the moment he had thrown himself into the water, the four had been watching carefully.

"He can't be in there, Frank, it's too narrow!" said Glenda shivering. The water was really cold, and they had been in it for too long.

Stella was going to add something, but suddenly, with a scream, Frank disappeared underwater.

"Frank!" yelled Stella.

Glenda and Rebecca started calling his name too, and tried to get to the point where their friend had been standing. They moved as fast as possible on the slippery ground. They got there panting, shivering for the cold and the shock. Suddenly, they saw a vortex appear in the water and felt its force between their legs.

"Here's what happened: here's the underground tunnel; the water flows through here, and if we get closer it will drag us down too", said Stella.

"What do we do now?" said Rebecca. "Maybe there's a way out from there, and Frank is a great swimmer…" she added, still crying. Then, as if in a trance, she threw herself into the vortex.

"Rebecca, no!" The two sisters tried to grab her by the arm, but she had already been sucked down by the water and, despite their efforts, they couldn't hold her back and ended up being dragged down as well. Stella barely had the time to shout that she couldn't swim.

A few endless moments passed, while the girls were dragged into the vortex that threw them all in the river below.

On the bank, they saw another cave, much bigger than the one they had just left. Even though the sunlight didn't arrive there, the hall was pervaded by a soft light, due to the fact that the rocky walls were covered with a luminescent substance.

"It must be a mushroom", Glenda muttered to herself while the river was dragging them all through a tunnel, where it got tighter and faster.

"Help! We're going down!" cried Stella. In the meantime, Rebecca had managed to grab Glenda's shirt, in the hope that contact would help them somehow.

The current dragged them on for about five minutes, and all along they kept screaming. Stella was struggling, trying to hold herself up the best she could. She was sure she was going to die. They had managed to survive falling from the balloon and Alfred's attack only to die drowned or smashed against one of those luminescent stalactites.

"Glenda! Rebecca! Try to grab me!" she screamed with all of her energies. If they were going to die, at least they'd die together.

When Rebecca and Glenda were pushed past her, Stella managed to grab her sister's arm. In that exact moment, the trio fell down a spectacular waterfall that left them breathless. A fall of about twenty meters and then *splash*, they were in a large pond. The tunnel ended with a natural fork due to a large stalactite that acted as a watershed: most of the water flew through a gully, while the rest formed the pond the girls had fallen in. Luckily the water was deep: otherwise they would have been really hurt, or worse.

They hadn't managed to keep clinging to one another. Before closing their eyes, the girls had enough time to look around and see that luminescence and some lights moving in the pond. They touched the bottom. Stella, who couldn't swim, moved her arms and legs so fast that she ended up being the first to resurface.

She gasped for a few minutes, her head spinning, then she felt someone grabbing her by the shoulders and cried out.

"It's me, Stella!" It was her sister who, along with Rebecca, was pushing her towards the shore.

"I thought it was one of those things down there..."

"Yes, we have seen them too. I wonder what they are, and what they eat", said Rebecca swimming and pushing, as fast as possible, Stella towards the shore.

They climbed on the rocks surrounding the pond and sat down, shivering, on a small patch of something that looked and felt like sand. The three girls remained in silence for a long time, as if they were recovering their physical and mental strength. Stella kept fidgeting with the sand, grabbing a handful and letting it fall through her fingers, like through an hourglass. Suddenly, the silence was broken by a voice behind them.

"I can't believe my eyes!"

Stella, Glenda and Rebecca, instead, couldn't believe their ears: it was Frank's voice.

"Frank! It's a miracle! We thought we had lost you forever! Come here!" They all hugged him, crying tears of joy.

Frank looked even more gaunt than usual: his clothes were still wet and he was freezing cold.

"I thought I'd never see you again... it really is a miracle..." he said.

Then he explained that he hadn't found any traces of Alfred although it was clear that, alive or dead, he had gone the same way they had.

"We saw some strange, luminescent creatures in the pond. Perhaps they have eaten him... " said Rebecca watching the water.

Frank suggested that it probably was simply some kind of fish, similar to those who live in the deep sea, where there's no sunlight. He didn't believe they were carnivores.

"They feed on algae or microorganisms", he explained: he had always been an avid reader of magazines about life in the deep sea.

Everything there seemed to resemble those depths: the only source of light was the fungi that covered the walls, the stalactites and the fish.

"I 've read just the opposite, Frank: most of the fish that live in the deep sea are carnivores", said Glenda, worried.

"Well, anyway, we aren't in the depths of the sea and those poor fish had to adapt somehow to the darkness of this cave", said Stella, trying to push away all the doubts and fears that her friends were feeling.

Frank reported that he had walked around and found the entrance to another cave where a very warm, strong wind was coming from. They decided to go that way to warm up and dry their clothes.

They walked around the pond and reached a large opening in the rock wall, opposite to the waterfall. Immediately they felt a warm gust. It wasn't a nice feeling: it was like having a hairdryer straight on their faces.

They went in. Stella wondered for how long they'd keep seeing those fungi that lit up that place, so fascinating and mysterious. The answer came almost immediately: they gave way to larger mushrooms the size of light bulbs, on the floor of the cave. Their interior was transparent and contained an iridescent substance that moved like a gas.

The air was hot and humid, and the four friends got immediately dry. Then, they started to sweat.

"Guys, let's go back. I don't like this place, I can't breathe... and I'm so thirsty I'd drink the whole pond dry!" complained Stella touching her throat. Her sister and Rebecca agreed with her; Frank, however, wanted to find out what was the source of that wind. He advanced, keeping an eye on the girls who had stopped near the entrance.

The boy slowly walked through a part of the cave where there were no mushrooms. The air grew even warmer, so much so that he took off his shirt and pants. He threw them on the ground and kept walking. The cave changed, there were quartz crystals everywhere. He arrived where the ceiling was higher. There, he heard a strange noise from behind a rock. It sounded like a fan. The scorching heat was almost unbearable. Frank leaned over the rock, and his face was hit by a gust of hot wind that made his hair stand. Instinctively, he pulled back and slipped, but he managed to hold on with his hands and didn't get hurt.

"Frank! What happened?" the girls asked.

"No problem, don't worry!" he replied. His words echoed around the cave.

He leaned slowly over the rock, just for a peek. To his amazement, he saw a hole nearly one meter across. It was dark inside, but in the distance he could see a yellow light, as big as a football.

What could it be? he wondered. He took a stone and threw it in to hear how deep it was. After a few seconds, the stone jumped back out and almost hit Frank in the face. "Damn!" he said, getting away fast.

The girls, who had watched the entire scene, begged him to get away from that place. "Let's go, Frank. This place is like Hell, and I'm feeling sick", Stella yelled.

The boy picked up his clothes, a piece of glass and some mushrooms, then he reached the girls. "I want to know what's in those mushrooms". Saying so, he handed two of them to Stella.

"Looks like an egg", she said, "and doesn't smell like a mushroom". She put it in a large pocket in her pants.

Frank told them what he had seen. Glenda explained that she had read a lot about the Apuan Alps, learning that they had emerged from the sea about 220 million years ago as a result of tectonic movements. That crater seemed to be magmatic and that yellow light was the proof of that. Who knows how deep it was, to look so small! Yes, no doubt that was the most likely explanation.

They got out of that cave and went back to breathe the fresh air and the oxygen produced by the great waterfall.

"How wonderful..." whispered Stella drinking from a stream of water coming down along the rock wall, near the pond. Suddenly, she let out a terrifying scream that startled Frank, Rebecca and Glenda.

"Not again!"

"Stella, what happened?" asked Frank, his voice broken by fear. He ran to her, followed by Glenda and Rebecca .

"This mountain is a graveyard", said the boy, disgusted.

Behind one of the rocks surrounding the pond, to Stella's left, there was a skull. It was buried from the nose down. Stella and Frank got closer, slowly. The boy prodded it with his right foot. He felt like an expert of skeletons. The skull was not attached to any body, because he rolled on the sand like a ball.

"How come this skull is here? Shouldn't it be attached to a neck and all the rest?" said Stella.

Frank dug a little trying to find something, but he had no luck: there was no trace of human bones, either there or in the surrounding area.

"Where is the rest of the body?" Glenda wondered. Rebecca, without saying a word, walked over to the pond and stared at the waters, so clean and so dark at the same time, lit only by some fish. The others understood what she was thinking about.

"True, perhaps the corpse is in the water, but still, we don't have any idea how his head got this far", said Frank, interpreting Rebecca's thoughts.

They decided to check. Stella wanted no part of it, as she couldn't swim. Rebecca, instead, was afraid of the fish. They decided that Frank and Glenda would take care of the situation: two are always better than one. Frank took the quartz crystal he had picked up in the warm cave and slipped it inside his shirt.

"We are not sure that those fish are harmless", he said ironically before diving into the dark waters with Glenda, near the spot where they had found the skull. The pond was shallow there, and they surfaced to breathe several times.

"There's nothing here!" Glenda gasped, ready to get out of the water.

Frank, instead, went down once again, where the water was deeper. The bottom was illuminated by a fish lying motionless on the sand. It looked like a monkfish, only much bigger. The boy went around it and noticed that, not far away, something was stuck amongst the algae. It looked like a piece of cloth. He pulled it, but it ripped; the part that remained in his hands looked a lot like something he had already seen. He tried to emerge in order to catch some breath but suddenly, while he was almost out, something grabbed his right foot. He shook his legs trying to get free, but couldn't. He felt his heart speeding up, and his ears seemed close to exploding.

He looked back, and what he saw attached to his foot terrified him: an eel-like creature had sunk its fangs into his shoe and was trying to drag him down. Frank grabbed the piece of glass and stabbed with it the head of the animal.

Meanwhile, Glenda, Stella and Rebecca, worried about him, begun to call his name: "Frank! What are you doing? Don't be silly, get out of the water!"

When they saw the boy pull his head out of the water gasping, clearly in trouble, they rushed to the pond, ignoring their fear of fish or the inability to swim.

They dragged him out of the water and made him lay on the sand. Frank hadn't dropped the piece of cloth he had found, and the fish hadn't left his foot. As soon as they saw that monster, the girls began to scream, but the boy managed to tell them that the beast was dead. Which was actually pretty plain to see, since its head was full of holes.

Stella, Glenda and Rebecca calmed down, and Frank rested for about ten minutes. Then he sat up and took off his shoe, the one targeted by the beast. He grabbed the fish's mouth and tried to open it, while the girls looked on with disgust.

"What kind of creature is that? I hope they can't leave the water", Stella commented, getting closer to the dead fish.

After freeing his shoe from the beast, Frank showed the girls the piece of cloth that he had found. It came from the shoulders of a military uniform that they had learnt to recognise easily: a German uniform from World War Two.

Of course, they couldn't understand how it had been torn to shreds and how the skull of the man who had likely worn it had ended up outside the pond.

"Sure the soldier got here the same way we did. But how come his head was in the sand and his uniform in the lake? Where's the rest of his body? I don't think these fish can leave the water and go hunt for food", concluded Glenda.

The four friends were sitting on the sand, their heads in their hands. They were in a place that felt hostile; also, it was dark and they didn't know how to get out. Also, they all were very hungry.

"I'm going to warm up, I'm cold now. We also need to find something to eat, I'm starving", said Frank standing up. He took the dead fish with him.

The girls understood where he was heading to, but didn't follow him: they were too tired.

At the entrance of the sauna-cave he took his clothes off, trying to think about a way to put the fish into the hot cave to cook it: the lower he'd dangle it, the better the hot air would have done the job. He thought about using his shirt, but it wasn't long enough; neither were his pants. While he was trying to find a solution, he heard Stella calling his name.

"Frank, are you here? We found something".

"I'm here, Stella", he replied. The girl showed him an old rope and a lantern similar to those they had found in the treasure cave.

"I bet they belonged to the man who wore the uniform", said Frank.

"And that head, I suppose", added Stella, handing him everything. The lantern would have been ideal to roast the fish, but they didn't have anything to light it. The rope, instead, would be good enough, even though it looked a little frayed.

Frank urged Stella to go back to the other girls with the lantern. The rope was about twenty meters long. He tied it to the tail of the fish and dangled it in the hot pit. He waited five minutes that felt like hours. He was breathing hard because of the heat, and felt his face and eyes were swelling. Then, slowly and carefully, he pulled up the rope. Dinner was ready!

He returned, tired but happy, to Stella, Glenda and Rebecca who, meanwhile, were trying to light up the lantern.

"The quartz!" said Stella. "Rubbing two pieces of quartz together can you get sparks!"

"Let's try!" said Glenda and Rebecca at the same time.

"Right!" said Frank picking up from the sand the piece of glass he had used to kill the fish. "Maybe we should enjoy the fish while it's still warm, though", he added.

"Yuck", said Stella. The other two girls seemed equally disgusted. Eventually, though, they decided to try it: they had no choice.

Frank cut the fish into strips with his crystal.

"Weird! It doesn't taste too bad. It's a bit like codfish stew", said Glenda, chewing as she stretched her hand to get another slice .

"A little more for me too, Frank. That monster was ugly but it tastes really good", added Stella, while Rebecca also asked for some more.

Stella stood up while eating the last of the fish. She walked towards the waterfall. She wanted to wash her hands and face in the fresh, clean water.

"Watch your step, Stella, the rocks are very slippery!" her sister said while washing her hands in the pond.

Stella leaned slowly towards the waterfall and felt the spray of the water on her face; she stretched her arms, the water running through her fingers. She seemed to feel it flowing in her mind too, and then she noticed something: a dark shadow on the wall. It was twice as tall as Frank and bigger than her. She couldn't see too well through the waterfall. She went even further, right next to the wall, and leaned on it, her left cheek touching the rock. She tried to observe the inner side of the waterfall to figure out where the shadow was coming from. She found a big crack.

"Come and see!" she yelled without moving her head.

Her friends, who were already watching her, asked: "What did you find? What is it?"

"I think that there is another cave here", she replied while sliding along the wall to the entrance.

Hearing her, Frank grabbed the lantern and the crystal.

"There's an entrance here, but it's too dark", Stella said, standing on the spot. Slowly, they all joined her. Frank moved where it was slightly drier.

"Wait, I'm trying to light up the lantern".

Saying so, he snapped the crystal in two, opened the lamp and started rubbing the quartz until the sparks ignited the wick.

"*Eureka*!" he shouted.

The oil began to burn. They could light up the dark cave. Of course Frank led the way. Every now and then, he stopped to check the ceiling of the cave. Then, suddenly, shedding light in front of himself, Frank jumped, followed by one of the girls saying: "No! I can't believe it!"

"What's that?"

Another skeleton!"

Indeed, a human skeleton was sitting against a wall. Its skull appeared larger than those they had seen before, and its clothes looked like bear skins. Its frontal lobes were also different from the others': they were much more prominent, and the big eye-sockets suggested ape-like features. After a pause of silence due to the surprise, Glenda spoke again: "Guys, I think this is a sensational discovery. We found the remains of a prehistoric man, I'm sure. On my science textbook there's a lot of photos of archaeological findings similar to this".

"Yes, and..." Frank didn't have time to finish what he was saying, as Stella interrupted him

"Look there! There's more!" she said, pointing her finger.

In a dark corner, they saw the skeletal fingers of two hands. And maybe there was even more.

Frank moved the lantern to light that corner and edged closer, followed by the others. This time, no one screamed or said anything: they were getting used to it.

"Two more here..." Stella muttered nonchalantly. Once they got near the two skeletons, they realised that something horrible had happened there.

"This is unbelievable", Rebecca said, while Stella and Glenda did their best not to scream.

Frank looked at what was left of those two human beings. They were both lying on the ground: one on its back and the other, who was much smaller, on its front. Clearly the latter was the skeleton of a child. The bigger skeleton was still holding a rotten, wooden spear with a stone tip.

What frightened the friends was the fact that the legs of the bigger skeleton were completely gone. This reminded them of the remains of the German soldier, who were still unaccounted for.

What a horrible creature could have done that? Was it possible that the same monster that had ripped the prehistoric man's legs off had done the same thing to the German soldier? All those questions were crowding their minds.

Frank sighed and said: "I think that, whatever did this, it can't be still alive. It's been at least sixty years since someone had walked in here. No living being can survive for so long without food".

"You forget about the fish…" Stella added. Glenda and Rebecca nodded.

"I didn't see any fish crawling out of the water!" said Frank ironically.

"Don't be silly!" said Rebecca. "Stella meant that the creature could have eaten the fish!"

"Ah, shut up! Something that eats fish won't eat human flesh", said Glenda.

"That's right, Glenda!" Frank confirmed. "I propose to stay here for a while. I don't know what time it is because my watch stopped, but I know I'm really tired". He yawned, putting the lantern on the floor.

"I don't know if I can sleep, even if I'm tired", said Rebecca. "My heart is still running fast, and the fact that we are in this 'merry company' certainly isn't helping. If we get out of here, I probably won't sleep for a week, because every time I'll fall asleep I'll wake up with nightmares!"

"Oh, please! We'll find a way to leave this place, you'll see, and in any case we've discovered something that we would never have imagined before. Think about it! People are going to space to discover new things, but we should watch closer", said Stella to make her feel better, even though in her heart she couldn't wait to leave.

They decided to get some rest there, as long as the lantern was still burning. They estimated that there was enough oil for at least four or five hours.

They sat down against the wall, to the left of the entrance of the cave.

Frank went back to the remains of the primitive men to take their bearskin clothes off; he did so slowly, to avoid breaking those fragile bones. Returning towards the girls, who looked at him with disappointment, he muttered under his breath: "It's not as if they still need them..."

They used them to avoid the feel of the cold stone against their backs. Frank fell asleep almost immediately while Rebecca, Stella and Glenda, although tired, couldn't sleep.

Stella stared into the darkness beyond the light of the lantern, and seemed to see something huge sway; she thought that her eyes were playing a trick on her, so she turned towards Frank, who was to her right, and closed her eyes. Then, slowly, she turned back and opened her eyes, but she saw nothing. "Thankfully, it was just an effect due to the low light", she thought. Then she turned again, first to look at her sister and Rebecca, who had already closed their eyes, and then to Frank. At the end, she tried to sleep.

She napped, but hers was not real sleep. Suddenly, she remembered about Alfred. What had happened to him? They hadn't found any trace of him. He could even be lurking somewhere in that strange "world", waiting for them, maybe with his dynamite, ready to blow everything and everyone up. While mulling over those things, she heard a sort of rustling, faint at first, then clearer. Stella was sure that it came from inside the cave. She held her breath to hear better. Something was crawling on the ground, against the rock. Panicked, she shook Frank awake. He opened his eyes and mouth to say something, but the girl, promptly, silenced him.

Stella looked into his eyes, gesturing to him to remain silent. That slithering noise continued, but they couldn't understand where it came from; then, suddenly, it stopped.

Stella woke up Rebecca and Glenda to get out of there but, as soon as the other two girls were awake, the head of a monstrous creature with a big grey crest appeared from the darkness, to their left. It looked like a dragon! Its eyes were on the sides of its head, covered by a thin white membrane suggesting that the creature was blind. Its nostrils and mouth also looked like a dragon's. Its teeth were sharp like knives. Then, it started growling. The sound was deafening.

A hot, smelly breath hit the faces of the four friends who, horrified, started crawling towards the exit of the cave after having thrown the bear skins in the mouth of the monster.

They ran out of the cave, slipping under the waterfall that hid the entrance, followed by the beast that, despite its blindness, had followed them: clearly, its sense of smell was very developed, and it had no intention of letting them go.

The friends didn't know where to hide, but Frank had an idea. While the girls ran toward the pond he headed back, running right in front of the dragon. The monster followed him towards the sauna-cave.

Frank ran inside, but started immediately feeling tired due to the heat. When he was just a few meters from the hole from which the heat came, he took off his sweaty shirt and threw it in. The dragon followed the scent of the boy's shirt, and remained stuck with its head inside the hot cavity. It roared in pain, writhing its monstrous body in an attempt to escape.

Frank ran towards the exit. The fatigue and the fear made him think that he could suffer a heart attack. As soon as he was in the bigger cave, he felt a wave of relief and began to breathe in the fresh air. That relief, however, soon turned into a shiver of cold, as he had used his shirt as a bait.

"Frank!" The girls ran to him. "Why did you do that? I was scared to death!" said his sister while the colour returned on the faces of their two friends.

Stella watched the boy's muscles, tuned by months of basketball training. Then she saw something more. The boy's tired face seemed heroic, and having defeated the dragon had made his eyes shine with a new light. His small pronunciation issue – he couldn't roll his R – started sounding attractive to her, and the retainer in his teeth faded to her eyes, becoming just a minor detail. It was as if she was looking at him for the first time.

"Where's your shirt? You'll catch a cold like that!" she said, trying to distract herself from those worrying thoughts.

"Where is that terrifying creature?" Glenda asked.

"I think we won't be seeing it for a long time, until we get out of here at least, and I hope that it happens as soon as possible", Frank said, shivering. "It has my shirt, but my vest should still be in the cave where we tried to sleep". Saying so, he ran to get it back.

He ran really fast: he really wanted to find a way out to escape from that place. He grabbed his vest and the lantern. On top of it, lying on the glass, he saw a strange insect. It looked like a mayfly, but it was larger and had a luminous body. As soon as Frank rose the lamp to watch it, the insect flew away towards the interior of the cave, where two or three others similar animals were flying. Then it disappeared.

The boy, intrigued, tried to reach the point where he had seen the insects. He walked on, illuminating with his lantern what looked like a graveyard: it was full of skeletons and carcasses of animals and humans. He was not impressed, because he knew that the author of that devastation was now roasting in a nearby cave. He kept walking until he found himself in front of something spectacular: a wonderful light came from the mouth of a tunnel. Frank gasped. He didn't know whether to proceed or not, but the attraction to the glow overcame him, so he did.

Thousands of those weird insects were illuminating a passage that lead upwards, in which some stone steps had been carved. They touched his face, hair and hands softly, with grace, without causing him any harm.

Frank decided to call the girls immediately: he was sure he had found the way out. He leaned out, over the waterfall, and let out a long whistle to attract their attention: they waiting near the pond. The girls turned. The boy gestured to join him.

"I found a way out!" Frank said with pride. "Come see!"

When his companions saw all those luminescent insects moving inside the passage, however, they refused to enter.

"No, no! I can't! Just the idea of feeling them crawl all over me makes me go crazy, they are everywhere", Rebecca whimpered.

"I'll cover my nose and ears. And I'd also need to sew my clothes on!" added Glenda.

"Are you kidding me? I can't... I'm nervous just seeing them", said Stella.

"They're harmless! I already tried", Frank reassured them. He went first and went up a step, being immediately hidden by thousands of those mayflies.

Stella was the first to follow him. She took a step up, closing her eyes in fear. She thought that the insects would creep all over her, but it didn't happen. She felt only slight caresses.

"It's true! They are harmless! They aren't bothering me at all", she said. Rebecca and Glenda braced themselves and followed.

They climbed those ancient stairs, lit by those mysterious insects that seemed to want to show them the way. Despite the staircase being long and steep, the friends did not feel any fatigue, as if those insects were having a beneficial effect on their physical strength.

"Look!" said Stella indicating a point from where some natural light seemed to be coming.

The mayflies seemed to refuse to fly where they could be hit by the light. The last ten steps were illuminated only by a soft light that penetrated through a hole, and were completely free from insects.

"Finally! Thank you!" said Stella, turning to those little creatures that had accompanied them up. But her joy faded when, unexpectedly, she hit something with her foot. It rolled down, ending on Frank's feet, two steps behind her.

"No way!" he muttered, picking up a stick of dynamite. Clearly Alfred was close by.

"Looks like someone's expecting us", he continued. He looked out and realized that they had returned to the main cave, on the other side of the pond. They had to face Alfred again.

"Nobody there", Frank whispered to his friends. They slipped out quickly. Stella rubbed her leg against a rocky outcrop, and the pocket that contained Frank's harvest tore. The mushrooms ended up on the floor and smashed.

"What a shame!" Stella said softly as the mushrooms began to exhale the luminescent substance they contained. They all bent down to observe the smoke. A strange dizziness started to invade them. Their heads were spinning, and everything around them seemed to be losing its edge.

Then Stella, somehow, found herself with the others in the cave where they had left the carpet. She started thinking that maybe it would be useful to get them out of there. It was a great opportunity to find out if the mythical flying carpet was just a legend or it really existed.

Suddenly they saw Alfred, who had lost the bag with the dynamite in the water and seemed to be looking for it. He was focussed on that task, so the friends still had some time.

"Here's the carpet! Let's take it before Alfred finds his dynamite!" Stella said.

They spread it on the rocky ground. It was beautiful! The design was gorgeous: it was the image of a forest full of deer and colourful butterflies. In the grass, there were strawberries. On the branches of a tree, that looked a lot like the chestnut tree where the Nautilus was entangled, was perched a big barn owl with its yellow eyes. The maker had represented the sky as well: on one side there was a big moon and some stars, on the other one the sun. The edge of the carpet was dotted with colourful flowers.

"Right, let's get on board", Stella said.

They sat down, in the middle of the carpet. They felt a little silly, but there was nothing else they could do. Frank and

Rebecca sat in front, Stella and her sister behind them. They remembered what the parchment said: they needed to use their imagination to make it fly.

"So, I will count to three and all together we'll focus on our wish to fly", said Frank.

As soon as he finished saying so, they heard Alfred yell: "Where are you? There's no way out! We'll remain here forever, buried with my treasure! Can you hear me?"

Rebecca and Frank counted to three: "One, two, three!" They closed their eyes, imagined to rise from the ground and, unexpectedly, the carpet really moved and began to rise and move forward.

"Hang on!" Frank said opening his eyes. Although they had nothing to hold on to except each other, they seemed stuck on the carpet, as if they had magnets in their pants. Stella tried to pull herself up, but she couldn't. A mysterious force kept them seated. They flew above Alfred's head. The man was open-mouthed, shocked by what he was seeing.

Rebecca and Frank bent to the left, and so did Stella and Glenda. The carpet veered, turning in circles. It changed direction following their movements!

When Alfred recovered from his astonishment, he threw a stick of dynamite towards them. To avoid it, the friends pulled back. The carpet went up, just in time to dodge the explosion that made some more stalactites fall.

The friends emerged like a missile from the large crack on the ceiling, and they were finally out of the hillock! They heard more explosions, and a white smoke started rising. They couldn't see anything.

When the breeze had blown the smoke away, they realised that only a few stones remained of the hillock: everything else had collapsed and caved in, sinking into the bowels of the earth.

Now they could go home! They already imagined the surprise of their parents and the people when they'd arrive riding the flying carpet.

Glenda remembered that the parchment said that the carpet would disappear at dusk, so they couldn't waste any time. They veered in the air and leaned forward to lower the flight. The carpet begun to glide quickly into the woods where they came from.

"We shouldn't go into the woods, Frank! We must continue down the valley!" Rebecca said. So the four pushed back, but probably they moved too briskly, due to their inexperience with flying carpets, and they turned upside down. They managed to hold on to their bags, but lost the sticks.

Even in those circumstances, the mysterious force that kept them attached to the carpet didn't fail, and they continued to fly, upside down, for several minutes. Unable to synchronise their movements, eventually they glided into the woods.

"Not again!" Stella cried. They started hitting the treetops and flew through the branches, covering their faces with their arms. Finally, the carpet dumped them on the grass, and they rolled for a few metres.

Stella was the first to recover. She stood, still bruised, her head spinning and her vision blurred. Then Frank, Rebecca and Glenda stood up too. They realized, all at the same time, they were still at the end of the tunnel, where the mushrooms had broken. "What happened? The flying carpet, the stick and..." Stella mumbled, dazed.

"The mushrooms, that's what! They are hallucinogenic! We had a hallucination", Glenda said, her head in her hands.

"Yes, it's true! I remember we were on a flying carpet, then we fell..." Rebecca confirmed, looking around. Frank added that surely it was a strong hallucinogen, most like the one contained in *Psilocybe Cubensis*, also known as Peyote; but he didn't think such a substance could give exactly the same vision to several people.

While they were still trying to understand what had happened, a big explosion startled them.

"You thought you could get rid of me? Poor children! Now you have no escape, the treasure will be mine!"

Alfred had reappeared with his dynamite, and this time it wasn't a dream: it was him, ready to make that cave their tomb. But he wasn't the only one who had some explosive: Frank still carried, in a pocket of his vest, the stick he had found on the steps of the secret passage.

They had a certain advantage over Alfred, who was still by the pond, so they decided to run to the exit. Their enemy had already blocked it, true, but Frank wanted to try to open a gate with the dynamite.

"Run, quick! Maybe we can blow up the boulders that block the entrance", said Frank, picking up his lantern. The girls followed him without saying a word.

Meanwhile, Alfred kept throwing dynamite and running behind them. "Where do you think you are going? Idiots!"

They reached the stones that separated them from freedom. "Hurry up, Frank!" yelled the girls, watching out for the madman.

The boy lit the fuse of the dynamite with the lantern and stuck it between the boulders. Then they huddled together and waited, covering their ears with the hands, for the dynamite to explode.

The explosion opened a little gap, large enough for them to pass one at a time.

As soon as they saw the sunlight coming in, they felt relieved. At the same time, they saw Alfred's dynamite a few feet away from them, its fuse quickly burning. The friends ran out, like ferrets, and rolled down the hillside, while the last explosion closed the access to that mysterious cave and its treasure forever.

Part of the hillock collapsed on itself, and white smoke rose up all around, just as they had seen in their hallucination. They gave one last look at that place and then, silently, they walked into the woods, with the hope of finding the tree where the Nautilus was still hanging on. That was the spot where the rescue team was most likely to be looking for them.

After half an hour walking among the chestnut trees... "Silence!" said Rebecca. "Listen!" In the distance, they heard a dog barking and a few voices. Finally, they had been found!

"We're here! This way!" they all shouted. The dog was the first one to reach them. Behind him came the rescuers.

"How are you? Are you okay?" asked one of them.

"We're fine, just a little tired and hungry", said Frank.

"I'm Dennis Romero, the leader of the rescue team. We have seen the Nautilus from the helicopter but, once in the woods, we couldn't find the exact spot. We got lost several times even if we are experts of the Apuan Alps, but finally, here you are!"

Another man came giving them some water and food. "You must be hungry after two days".

The four friends told them that they had been feeding on berries and drinking water from a mountain spring. They said they didn't know what had happened to their pilot, whom they hadn't seen him since the balloon fell.

They set off on the way back along with the rescuers, who gave them waterproof jackets to warm up. They heard them tell their base that they had found the four lost teenagers, and that they were fine.

They'd never tell anyone what had really happened, because they knew that their story would attract too many curious people on Mount Tambura, ruining the place and scaring away the animals that lived there. As for the treasure, they were glad that it was now buried forever. They wondered how many people had suffered because of that gold.

They felt sorry for Alfred, but there was nothing they could do for him: he had fallen victim of his own greed.

Frank, Rebecca, Stella and Glenda only kept two golden coins, one for each family, promising that they'd try to use them in the best possible way.

Stella, who dreamed to become a writer, now had a fantastic story to tell.

Titolo | The ballon, Mount Tambura and the Flying
Carpet Autore | Fernanda Raineri

ISBN | 978-88-91172-93-8

Youcanprint Self-Publishing
Via Roma, 73 – 73039 Tricase (LE) – Italy
www.youcanprint.it
info@youcanprint.it
Facebook: facebook.com/youcanprint.it
Twitter: twitter.com/youcanprintit

9 788889 117293